*Acting Edition*

# I'll Never Love Again

## by Clare Barron

SAMUEL FRENCH

**FOR PRODUCTION INQUIRIES**

UNITED STATES AND CANADA
info@concordtheatricals.com
1-866-979-0447

UNITED KINGDOM AND EUROPE
licensing@concordtheatricals.co.uk
020-7054-7298

Each title is subject to availability from Concord Theatricals Corp., depending upon country of performance. Please be aware that *I'LL NEVER LOVE AGAIN* may not be licensed by Concord Theatricals Corp. in your territory. Professional and amateur producers should contact the nearest Concord Theatricals Corp. office or licensing partner to verify availability.

No one shall make any changes in this title(s) for the purpose of production. No part of this book may be reproduced, stored in a retrieval system, scanned, uploaded, or transmitted in any form, by any means, now known or yet to be invented, including mechanical, electronic, digital, photocopying, recording, videotaping, or otherwise, without the prior written permission of the publisher. No one shall share this title(s), or any part of this title(s), through any social media or file hosting websites.

For all inquiries regarding motion picture, television, online/digital and other media rights, please contact Concord Theatricals Corp.

## MUSIC AND THIRD-PARTY MATERIALS USE NOTE

Licensees are solely responsible for obtaining formal written permission from copyright owners to use copyrighted music and/or other copyrighted third-party materials (e.g. artworks, logos) in the performance of this play and are strongly cautioned to do so. If no such permission is obtained by the licensee, then the licensee must use only original music and materials that the licensee owns and controls. Licensees are solely responsible and liable for clearances of all third-party copyrighted materials, including without limitation music, and shall indemnify the copyright owners of the play(s) and their licensing agent, Concord Theatricals Corp., against any costs, expenses, losses and liabilities arising from the use of such copyrighted third-party materials by licensees. For music, please contact the appropriate music licensing authority in your territory for the rights to any incidental music.

## IMPORTANT BILLING AND CREDIT REQUIREMENTS

If you have obtained performance rights to this title, please refer to your licensing agreement for important billing and credit requirements.

*I'LL NEVER LOVE AGAIN* received its world premiere at The Bushwick Starr (Noel Allain, Artistic Director; Sue Kessler, Executive Director) in New York City with an opening night of February 24, 2016. The production was directed by Michael Leibenluft and the Composer and Music Supervisor was Orion S. Johnstone. The set design was by Carolyn Mraz with costume design by Karen Boyer, sound design by Gareth Hobbs, and lighting design by Mary Ellen Stebbins. The Music Director was Kailey Marshall. The Production Manager was Ann Marie Dorr, the Technical Director was Jen Medina-Gray, and the Producer was John Del Gaudio. The Production Stage Manager was Taylor Wilkerson, and the Assistant Stage Manager and Dramaturge was Sophie Weisskoff. The Assistant Director was Emily Moler. The cast was as follows:

**ONE/AMANDA** . . . . . . . . . . . . . . . . . . . . . . . . . . . . . . . . . . . . . . . Kate Benson

**TWO/JACKSON** . . . . . . . . . . . . . . . . . . . . . . . . . . . . . . . . . . Peter Mills Weiss

**THREE** . . . . . . . . . . . . . . . . . . . . . . . . . . . . . . . . . . . . . . . . . Mia Katigbak

**FOUR/CLARE** (Lawyer Scene) . . . . . . . . . . . . . . . . . . . . . . . Nana Mensah

**CLARE** (Sex Scene) . . . . . . . . . . . . . . . . . . . . . . . . . . . . . . . . Clare Barron

**GUY** . . . . . . . . . . . . . . . . . . . . . . . . . . . . . . . . . . . . . .Paul Cameron Hardy

**ROGER** . . . . . . . . . . . . . . . . . . . . . . . . . . . . . . . . . . . . . . . . .Richard Toth

**OONA** . . . . . . . . . . . . . . . . . . . . . . . . . . . . . . . . . . . . . . . .Oona Montandon

**CHOIR** . . . . . . . . . . . . . . . . . . . . .Joie Bauer, Amanda Phelan, Jeremy Rafal,
Maggie Robinson, Brittane Rowe,
Shawn Shafner, & Kailey Marshall

# CHARACTERS

**ONE/AMANDA**
**TWO/JACKSON**
**THREE**
**FOUR/CLARE** – (lawyer scene)
**CLARE** – (sex scene)
**GUY**
**ROGER**
**OONA**
**CHOIR A–G**


# AUTHOR'S NOTES

This piece is to be performed by a diverse ensemble of all ages. All genders, all races, all backgrounds, all bodies, all sexualities, all souls.

The performers labeled **ONE**, **TWO**, **THREE**, and **FOUR** are our main ensemble who will lead us through the show. They are part of a twelve-person choir, and they emerge slowly from the choir over the course of the piece.

The characters of **CLARE** and **GUY** in the sex scene are played by members of the choir. (And in the premiere production, the character of **CLARE** in the sex scene was played by the "historical" Clare, i.e., me.)

The character of **CLARE** in the office scene is played by the performer playing **FOUR**. The character of **AMANDA** in the office scene is played by the performer playing **ONE**. And the character of **JACKSON** in the office scene is played by the performer playing **TWO**.

**ROGER** and **OONA** are new actors, not in the choir, who appear for the first time in the office scene. **OONA** should be played by a real thirteen-year-old.

***

In Acts One–Three (the choral section), capitalized text is sung.

***

Text in Acts One–Three is taken from my actual teenage diary (circa 2000–2004)

# NOTE ON MUSIC

Sheet music for the songs "Loch Lomond", "Why Are You Not With Me?", "Have You Ever?", "The Hurt", and "Wayfaring Stranger (Apocalypse Version)", composed and arranged by Orion S. Johnstone, is required for production. Sheet music for "Angels We Have Heard On High" is not included, however licensees may use any arrangement that is in the public domain. Please refer to your performance license for important credit requirements and more information.

*The lights are up. The house lights are on. We see people in choir robes ambling and then scurrying to get into place backstage.*

*The show's about to start!*

*The lights go dim. Then black.*

*Someone enters. They're wearing a beautiful, ancient, purple-and-gold choir robe.*

*They begin. Very thoughtful and simple.*

**THREE.** I no longer think it's disgusting to think about kissing him. When did that happen? I don't know. I used to think I liked him. And then I would close my eyes and I would think about kissing him. And it would gross me out. So I thought: Okay. I must not like him. One time we lay on the carpet and touched each other's fingers. And that was nice. But any thoughts about his lips. Or us being lip-to-lip. Or his face that close to my face...

> *They make a face.*

I don't know. I just find it disgusting. Like his mouth on my mouth? *His mouth on my mouth?* Joshua Wilson's mouth on my mouth?

> *They shrug.*

I don't know. I just find the thought of it revolting. Really really really really really really really really really really really really really really really really really really really really really revolting.

**THREE**.  Or… I guess I *found* it revolting. I now find it *slightly* less revolting. Which is not to say that I *want* to kiss him. Just that I have woken up from several dreams where he was holding me in his arms, and I felt quite comfortable and safe. And now when I close my eyes and think about kissing him. It's slightly less gross.

> *They close their eyes. They think about kissing Josh…*

> *A whole army of people enter. They parade onto the risers, surrounding speaker THREE. They're all in choir robes. They are all playing "CLARE."*

> *They all close their eyes. They think about kissing Josh…*

…

…

…

> *Opening their eyes…*

**THREE**.  Yup. Slightly less gross.

> *The CHOIR breathes, focuses, gets very quiet…*

> *The concert begins.*

## [MUSIC NO. 01 – LOCH LOMOND]

**ALL.**

BY YON BONNIE BANKS AN' BY YON BONNIE BRAES
WHAUR THE SUN SHINES BRIGHT ON LOCH LOMON'
WHAUR ME AN' MY TRUE LOVE WILL NE'ER MEET AGAIN
ON THE BONNIE, BONNIE BANKS O' LOCH LOMON'.
O YE'LL TAK' THE HIGH ROAD, AN' I'LL TAK' THE LOW ROAD
AND AH'LL BE IN SCOTLAND AFORE YE
FIR ME AN' MY TRUE LOVE WILL NE'ER MEET AGAIN

ON THE BONNIE, BONNIE BANKS O' LOCH LOMON'.
'TWAS THERE THAT WE PERTED IN YON SHADY GLEN
ON THE STEEP, STEEP SIDES O' BEN LOMON'
WHAUR IN (SOFT) PURPLE HUE,
THE HIELAN HILLS WE VIEW
AN' THE MOON COMIN' OOT IN THE GLOAMIN'.
O YE'LL TAK' THE HIGH ROAD, AN' I'LL TAK' THE LOW
   ROAD
AND AH'LL BE IN SCOTLAND AFORE YE
FIR ME AN' MY TRUE LOVE WILL NE'ER MEET AGAIN
ON THE BONNIE, BONNIE BANKS O' LOCH LOMON'.

*The following is underscored by music...*

**ONE.**

...
...
...
...
...
...

I saw him at the choir concert. He's in the senior choir. I'm in the sophomore choir. It's embarrassing to be in the sophomore choir because we're not that good. The senior choir gets to wear gowns and tuxedos. We have to wear robes. Like we're in church.

...
...
...
...

Anyway, Josh was sitting in the audience in his tuxedo and I was onstage in my robe and I looked out and I saw him sitting with *my coat* on *his lap.*

...
...

*(WHAT THE FUCK!!!!!)*

...
...

And I almost forgot all the words to the song

...
...
...
...
...

And then afterwards he came up to me and told me good job and handed me my coat and said that I'd left it backstage. And *then* he said:

...
...
...

*(Trying hard to remember his exact words/slightly still in disbelief that he actually said this.)*

**ONE.**

... I could smell your smell on your coat so it
... was almost like... I was sitting *right next to*
... *you* at the concert.

...

... *(HOLY SHIT!!!!!)*

...

... And then he handed me back the coat and
... kind of kind of touched me on my side like
... this...

...

... *(They all touch themselves on*
... *their sides and remember that*
... *touch...)*

...

...

... And said:

...

... **ALL.**

... How are you doing, Clare?

...

... **ONE.**

... And when he touched me like that on my
... side it was like roots sprung up out of the
... ground and grew up both my legs and
... through my whole body and then a tree
... came out of my head and exploded into a
... lightning bolt.

...

**CHOIR A.**

THE WEE BIRDIES SING AN' THE WILD FLOWERS SPRING
AN' IN SUNSHINE THE WATERS ARE SLEEPIN'
BUT THE BROKEN HEART IT KENS, NAE SECOND SPRING
    AGAIN
THO' THE WAEFUL MAY CEASE FRAE THEIR WEEPIN'...

...
...
...
...
...
...

**CHOIR B.**

The next time I interacted with him was at the sophomore Valentine's Day dance. We danced around a pole and he handed me a paper heart from the decorations.

He was dating Aly at that time. She was the nicest and prettiest girl at school. I was at the dance grooving with Beka, and I look over and I see him bouncing straight up and down, over-and-over again, and with each bounce he's saying my name: Clare! Clare! Clare! Clare! He wanted to dance with me. I was shy-slash-embarrassed, and asked Aly if it would be okay. She laughed. I danced with him and the mixture of his sweat and cologne gave me a rash on my forearm.

**CHOIR C.**

Six weeks later Aly had broken up with him and he was heartbroken. I ran into him at the Spring Fling. My hair was cut short and shaggy and I was slightly broken out and self-conscious. He literally *grabbed me* by the arm and *physically moved* me while Seth held Beka back. He told me that the Valentine's Day dance was his favorite dance he'd ever been to and it was because he had danced with me. I laughed and awkwardly said "Thank you" and gave him a hug and turned and ran the opposite direction. I've kicked myself a thousand times for that one.

...

I thought it meant that he would ask me to Prom...

... **CHOIR B.**
...       Too late. Phoebe asked him a week before
...       the dance (the night of the soccer game
...       when I touched his scar).
...

... **ONE.**
...       The day of Prom really sucked. Audrey told
...       me that her aunt had attempted suicide
...       the night before, my French teacher had a
...       personal emergency, I forgot my planner
...       at home, I got a lot of homework, I didn't
...       understand the math, I found out Mr.
...       Lorenson scheduled our final bio test for
...       the last day of school, Mr. Jackson told
...       me that I had to miss ballet for the choir
...       concert, they want to take me out of the
...       coolest dance sequence in the musical
...       because I have to change my costume, and
...       nobody asked me to Prom so I'm not going.

...       ...
...       I was depressed and Josh kept asking me
...       what was wrong and to tell "Uncle Josh"
          and I wanted to scream at him that he's not
          my uncle!!!!

**ALL.** *(The big finale.)*

O YE'LL TAK' THE HIGH ROAD, AND AH'LL
    TAK' THE LOW ROAD
AN' I'LL BE IN SCOTLAND AFORE YE
FIR ME AN' MY TRUE LOVE WILL NE'ER
    MEET AGAIN
ON THE BONNIE, BONNIE BANKS O' LOCH
    LOMON'!

*Applause. They beam out at the audience.*

**TWO.** I never got a sex talk. My siblings were all enlightened with help from a disturbingly graphic "naked people" book from the 1970s when they were *eleven*. But I think my mom must have forgotten about me…

**CHOIR D.**

I found it last summer in the basement.

Opened it up and saw a bunch of headless, nude male bodies – their little men just dangling.

**CHOIR E & A.**

Scary.

**CHOIR F.**

Naked men are scary.

**ONE.**

I'm sorry but Mr. Penis is not exactly a pretty sight. Why I'm supposed to be attracted to a lumpy, hairy, fleshy cucumber, I'll never know.

**CHOIR D.**

I will confess that I find testicles fascinating, however. The way they hang outside the body.

**CHOIR F.**

96.6° Fahrenheit. Perfect temperature for manufacturing sperm.

**CHOIR D.**

Vas deferens tubes coiled up inside…

**CHOIR E.**

I always imagine them grey. I don't know why.

**CHOIR A.**

I want to cup them in my hand and lift them. Free them from gravity.

**CHOIR E.**

Bounce them up and down slowly.

> **CHOIR B.**
> Put them in my mouth (although I'm not
> exactly sure how that works...)
>
> **THREE.**
> I want to inspect a man the way I poke and
> pick at an ugly scab.

**TWO.** I'm a lot of talk, though. Scared is what I am. I like to do things I know how to do and can do well and I am definitely sexually clueless and clumsy. Well alright. Sometimes an inner tiger emerges. But frankly, if pants were to ever...

**THREE.** (and we're talking in the *faaarrrr* future)

**TWO.** ...were to ever come off, I would be lost. And reluctant.

And maybe that's a good thing? Because I think I want to wait.

> **CHOIR E.**
> Wait for what?
>
> **CHOIR F.**
> My whole life is waiting!

**TWO.** Wait for a husband! A long-term boyfriend!

**THREE.** A nameless specimen I meet on a beach!

**TWO.** I just know that if I give it away too early or based on lust or just because I'm particularly horny as opposed to true, committed love...

*They all chant:*

**I WOULD HATE MYSELF.**
**NEVER FORGIVE MYSELF**
**FEEL DIRTY**
**WANT OUT OF MY BODY**
**MENTALLY PUNISH MYSELF OVER-**
**AND-OVER AGAIN FOR THE REST OF**
**MY LIFE**

**THREE.** Also? It must be perfect.

It must be more than I ever expected/dreamed/fantasized/heard about.

It must be genuine and honest.

**ALL.** It must be me – Clare!

**THREE.** Truly *MAKING LOVE* and not some part I'm playing to please somebody else or do what's expected of me.

**ONE.** That summer I finally got up the courage to call Josh on the phone. It was the first time I'd ever called a boy for pure conversation. We talked about baby chickens. It was..............................................................................................................A THRILL. He asked if I wanted to hang out. I went over to his house. Over to his *room*. I remember studying the posters on his wall. A question for every poster. And I squirmed. I had so much excited energy in me, I couldn't keep still. I crawled up and down him. Flipped off the bed. Mauled his head. At one point he may have even smacked my.................................butt. It happened so fast and I was so shocked. I'm not sure.

**THREE.** I thought maybe he'd invite me to spend the Fourth of July together...

**ONE.** He didn't. And he didn't call me back all summer

### FOUR.

Sometimes I just want to whisper. It makes
me feel like I have a secret. I want to invite
someone over for tea and make it really slowly
and carefully...cautiously...like I'm thinking of
something heavy. Then I want to pour them
a *hot drink* and just when the china reaches
their lips, I'll lean in......and......*whisper*

((((*The British
have landed*))))))

**FOUR.**
Or I don't know what I'll say, I could say
anything! I just want to feel like I'm full of
secrets...

**ONE.**  I think in October he came over to my house. I was
in my basement sorting through the chest of drawers.
Cleaning. Alone. I think it was a Tuesday. I was wearing
my high-waisted khaki shorts and the striped V-neck
hand-me-down from Andrea. He came, and I changed
into new jeans and the two-button salmon/pink shirt
(the one that spontaneously comes unbuttoned). He
took me to a harvest festival at The Jacksons'. We
walked through the orchard together. It was getting
dark, and at some point I wandered away from him
and then couldn't find him again, and it just got darker
and darker and darker and darker...

**TWO.**  And then I heard something moving behind me in
the trees...

**ONE.**  And then it ran towards me – full-speed – and body-
slammed me to the ground.

**TWO.**  And it was Josh. He just lay there on top of me.
He didn't move or talk or anything.

**ONE.**  His full weight on top of me, like he was dead.

**TWO.**  I could've stayed under him forever.

**ONE.**  And I could smell him. And it made me feel like an
animal

**TWO.**  And *still* we didn't date for two months. And *still* I
wasn't sure he liked me.

**FOUR.**  Beka told me that it's good to write down your
limits so that you're less tempted to cross them so
I made this list:

      **CHOIR A.**
         (1) I will not take my pants off with a boy

**CHOIR E.**

(2) I will not take my underwear off with a boy

**THREE.**

(3) A boy can stick his hand down my underwear but he cannot take them off

**CHOIR A.**

(4) I can take off my shirt

**FOUR.**

(5) But not my bra

**CHOIR G.**

(6) A boy can stick his hand under my bra but he cannot take it off

**ONE.** After the harvest festival, Josh drove me home, and in the car he whispered to me that I was beautiful and I pretended not to hear.

**FOUR.**

(7) I will not do anything to disrespect my parents

**CHOIR D.**

(8) I will not do anything that will put me in physical and/or emotional danger

**ONE.** And then on December twenty-third he invited me over to his room. In the basement. And we read Christmas stories. And then he kissed me. Like this.

*They all demonstrate a very simple open-mouthed (but no tongue) kiss on their hands.*

**ONE.** And then he kissed me again. And then again. Three times. And then he drove me home. And I had Christmas with my family... And it was the most beautiful Christmas ever.

**[MUSIC NO. 02 – ANGELS WE HAVE HEARD ON HIGH]**

**CHOIR.**
> ANGELS WE HAVE HEARD ON HIGH
> SWEETLY SINGING O'ER THE PLAINS
> AND THE MOUNTAINS IN REPLY
> ECHOING THEIR JOYOUS STRAINS...
> GLORIA IN EXCELSIS DEO
> GLORIA IN EXCELSIS DEO
> COME TO BETHLEHEM AND SEE
> CHRIST WHOSE BIRTH THE ANGELS SING
> COME ADORE ON BENDED KNEE
> CHRIST THE LORD THE NEWBORN KING
> GLORIA IN EXCELSIS DEO
> GLORIA IN EXCELSIS DEO

## CURTAIN. END OF ACT I

## ACT II

### TWO.

> Romance is dead. Romance is dead for me FOREVER. He kissed me and nothing happened. I thought it was supposed to be fireworks. I thought the Earth was supposed to move. I thought *your first kiss* was supposed to feel *different* or *big* or something or anything special. But it was just lips-against-lips. It was just two mouths touching. It was nothing special at all.

**THREE.** The second time he kissed me it was on my front porch. A little wetter this time. A little wetter and a little colder. It was cold outside and his mouth was cold.

**ONE.** The third time he kissed me it was in his backyard in a hammock. It was snowing. We were both in snowsuits. And I lay on top of him like a pancake on top of another pancake and we kissed. Many times. And snowflakes landed on his face.

**THREE.** The fourth time he kissed me was when I went with him to the eyeglasses shop to get new glasses. And I was giving him my opinion on what looked good. And the eyeglass lady asked: Is this your girlfriend? And he looked at me. And he said: YES. And then we kissed in his car in the parking lot.

**ONE.** The fifth time he kissed me was in my driveway in his car. My mom came out to say hello and when she walked up I was sucking Josh's fingers. It was incredibly embarrassing.

**THREE.** The sixth time he kissed me we were with a group of friends. And I did something funny. And he kind of grabbed me and kissed me on the side of my face. It made me feel so...............loved.

**ONE.** Those were the first six times we kissed. I used to go through all our kisses in bed at night before I fell asleep. And even remembering them made me feel kind of sick inside. But in a good way. And then after awhile I started losing track. It made me so sad to lose track. I wanted to remember every single kiss. I was so scared of forgetting them. But then I was like: Clare. Just live your life. You have to let it go.

**TWO.** I want to see you tomorrow. I want to talk to you. I want to be with you tonight. I want to feel open next to you and naked next to you. I want to be exposed in your presence. Raw in your presence. I want you to hold a knife to my throat. I want to reach inside you. Crawl inside you. Sleep inside your flesh. Breathe through your mouth, your nostrils, feel your chest rise and fall as you sigh.

**THREE**.  I want to talk to you. And I don't want to talk. I want to tell you a lot. But I need to write it on your skin, with my pulse.

### [MUSIC NO. 03 – WHY ARE YOU NOT WITH ME?]

...

WHY AM I SO STILL TONIGHT?

...

WHY AM I SO SAD TONIGHT?

...

WHY AM I DEPLETED TONIGHT?

...

How is it already eleven o'clock?

...

HOW WILL I SLEEP TONIGHT?

...

**ONE OTHER VOICE**.
WHY AM I SO STILL TONIGHT?

...

WHY AM I SO SAD TONIGHT?

**THREE**.
WHY ARE YOU NOT WITH ME?

**ONE OTHER VOICE**.
WHY AM I DEPLETED TONIGHT?

...

**TWO VOICES**.

WHY ARE YOU NOT WITH ME?

...

**FOUR VOICES.**

WHY ARE YOU NOT WITH ME?

**FOUR.**

You are a turkey foot

By which I mean I want to gnaw on your bones

By which I mean I want to gnaw your bone

By which I mean I want to squeeze you tight

By which I mean I think you're alright

By which I mean I love you with all my might

**THREE.**

WHY AM I SO STILL
TONIGHT?
WHY AM I SO SAD
TONIGHT?
WHY AM I DEPLETED
TONIGHT?
WHOA WHOA

**FOUR VOICES.**

WHY ARE YOU NOT WITH ME?

WHY ARE YOU NOT WITH ME?

**TWO.**

I'm sorry I called you when you needed sleep. I'm sorry I didn't have the sense not to get lost. I'm sorry if I'm always dragging you down. I want to be a better girlfriend. I'm sorry that my problems and complexes end up negatively affecting you. I wish I were well-adjusted and easygoing...............

**CHOIR C & D.**

I hope you have fun in the snow tomorrow.

**ONE.**  Probably about halfway through our relationship. We were at his house and his twin sister Megan was upset because Marcus had kissed a rotary exchange student from Brazil. Josh and I were stuck downstairs waiting for Marcus to tell us that it was safe to come up. I taped Josh's eyes shut with scotch tape and ran in circles while he tried to catch me. That night I was wearing the red/purple/green/white/black-striped shirt that was Sarah's in Elementary School. We talked about many things. I made him tell me the three boys he would most hate for me to kiss.

**TWO.**  (Paul, Scott, and Mystery Man).

**ONE.**  And I told him mine.

**THREE.**  (Aly, Brittany, and Brie).

**ONE.**  We laughed and kissed. Me on top of him with my hair fanned out to make a hiding place waiting for his long lashes to close so that I could open my eyes and study his sweet, sweaty face.

We kissed long but soft and patient. Content and comfortable. And Marcus yelled at the top of the stairs: STOP MAKING OUT

### [MUSIC NO. 04 – HAVE YOU EVER?]

*She laughs. This is the best.*

**ONE.**  Stop making out!

**CHOIR.**
HAVE YOU EVER REALLY QUESTIONED
THE EXISTENCE OF GOD? HAVE YOU EVER
HAD NIGHTS WHERE YOUR HEART BREAKS
SPONTANEOUSLY?

**ONE.**  One time I had a fever and it was Valentine's Day and we were making out in the wicker room (the room in his house entirely full of wicker furniture) my shirt came unbuttoned and I let him touch my breasts.

**CHOIR.**

HAVE YOU EVER BELIEVED IN THE MAYAN
APOCALYPSE? TWO-THOUSAND-TWELVE! DO
YOU EVER HAVE PROBLEMS FALLING ASLEEP?

**THREE.**  And another time we were making out on the top of a water tower and Zach was there playing guitar. And then Zach left. And it was just the two of us. And it looked like we were in Bethlehem or something. I don't know why. It just looked Biblical with the grass and the hills and the little white houses and being in a sleeping bag outside and he took off my bra and he saw my breasts and afterwards he asked me if I was okay.

...

...

...

...

...

...

**FOUR.**  Sometimes I just want to *<she screams>*

I just feel so much I just want to *<she screams>*

Like I listen to music in my head and I just want to *<she screams>*

I just feel so sexy

I feel myself dancing

I'm like dancing and sexy and just like *<she screams>*

And he wants me so much

He wants me so, so much

Everyone wants me so, so much

I wait for him to come pick me up in his car and I just run around the house because I'm so full of *<she screams>* and so excited

**TWO**.  And sometimes. He'd put his hand down my shirt and try to find my heartbeat...? Like this

*They all demonstrate.*

**ONE, TWO & THREE**.  It was like our thing.

**FOUR**.  I get scared sometimes that I'll get so desperate or angry or hurt or horny that I'll just go for it in the moment. The animal part of me rebelling against the spiritual. Nature screaming: MAKE BABIES! TAKE THE SPERM! TAKE THE SPERM! WANT THE SPERM! MAKE THE BABIES! It's a trap. A positive-feedback loop like in biology. You get on the water slide and there's no climbing back up, you know what I'm saying? You've got to go all the way down to the splash. You can try and put your legs and arms out and stop yourself from sliding but then you're just stuck there halfway down the slide the water pushing past you.

**THREE**.  Friggin Mother Nature! My sexual cheerleader.

**FOUR**.  Take your shirt off, Clare! Grab him! Kiss him! Press closer! You're hungry, Clare! Do you feel the intensity of your hunger?? He's the feast! Go for it! Don't be afraid! Taste him! Eat him! Eat him! And I go numb and burn and my body switches sides. I'm no longer in control. My body aligns with nature moving faster than my mind can control or formulate rebuttals and I'm screwed – literally and figuratively – and I love it! I love losing control, floating, letting forces greater than myself take over, being part of it all, being part of nature, being a woman...

**THREE**. But...

**FOUR**. But...

**ONE**. But.........................................

**FOUR**.  I know if I give up my virginity too soon (and yes, maybe I'm wasting precious years of life, maybe I'm dulling the vibrancy of everything) I would regret it.

**THREE**.  I would regret it. And hate myself.

**ONE**.  I would regret it. For the rest of my life.

**TWO**.  The last time we hung out before he dumped me, we returned the motorcycle helmets that we borrowed from Mr. Jackson for our astronaut costumes for the Spring Fling. Mr. Jackson fed us soup and ice cream and we secretly touched on the couch. But Josh didn't want to go to Dry Falls with me, and it was a beautiful day. He didn't want to play outside. He was tired and boring.

**THREE**.  We sat in St. Joseph's parking lot staring at an ugly bush while birds chirped. A nun came outside. We sat – I leaned on him – and didn't talk. I was tired of dragging the conversation. Tired of trying to be interesting.

**TWO**.  I contemplated kissing him...

**THREE**.  And then didn't.

**TWO**.  I was lazy. And besides – the nuns were watching.

   ...

   ...

   ...

## [MUSIC NO. 05 – THE HURT]

**ONE**.  And then it was over. He drove me to his house and we sat in his room in the basement. It took two hours for him to break up with me. I didn't understand what was happening or what he was talking about. And then finally I said: Are you breaking up with me? And he said yes.

   ...

   ...

   ...

And then when he went to the bathroom I stole this T-shirt.

*FOUR pulls a T-shirt out of their pants.*

**FOUR.** It was dirty and on the floor and I took it so I could remember his smell.

*FOUR smells it.*

**FOUR.** But then later I felt guilty about it and so I cut out the tag and returned the shirt and kept the tag in a special little treasure box alongside my baby teeth

*Music! The CHOIR sings their bruised, bloody hearts out. An anthem called "The Hurt."*

**CHOIR.** *

I AM UPROOTED.
I AM BEATEN.
I AM BRUISED.
I AM DYING.
IF THIS IS THE WAY IT'S GONNA BE…
THEN I DON'T WANT TO DO IT AT ALL.
I DON'T WANT TO DO THIS EVER AGAIN.

## CURTAIN. END OF ACT II

## ACT III

**TWO.** I have a medicine that helps me sleep. Except sometimes when I take it, I still can't fall asleep. And it makes me extremely nauseous. It drains all the blood from my face, and if I get up in the middle of the night, it's as if someone's cut slits in the bottom of my feet and all the blood flows out and pools around my feet and I have to lie on the floor to soak it back up and my face is cold and white and made of clay

---

* Please refer to the score for the full set of lyrics to this song.

**FOUR.** It's the week before Prom when Josh breaks up with me and he ends up asking someone else to the dance and I stay home and study for the SAT.

**ONE.** Two years in a row. No Prom for me.

**FOUR.** I see him walking down the hallway between periods two and three and I panic and as I pass him I put my finger in my eye (I don't know why) and he looks at me like I'm a crazy person.

**THREE.** I break out so bad that I feel like a monster and I stay home from school. The next day I wear this skirt from seventh grade. I bought it in San Francisco with my mom. It's light blue and kind of fuzzy with tiny tiny sparkles woven into the fabric that look like tiny tiny tinsel. It's too small on me and really really tight across my butt. Before choir I'm hanging out in the music department and the older boys are there. And Josh too. And this guy Top keeps looking at my butt. And then he says: Sorry. You have a really nice butt. And then *Josh* says: Yeah. She has a really amazing butt. And then I say: Yeah but I don't have any boobs.

And then Josh *doesn't say anything*.......... He's just quiet.

And *then* he says: You have.........very...nice...breastsss.

And in that pause in that pause is *infinite humiliation.* Because he's lying. I can tell that he is lying. He thinks my breasts are ugly. He thinks my breasts are *not awesome.* He hates my breasts. And for the first time I think: my body is not good enough. My body is not as good as other bodies. My breasts are not good enough.

...

...

...

I always thought that "sexy" was just a feeling. It was something I felt. But now I know it's something I am. Or I am not. And I don't get to decide.

**ONE**. It's the end of the year assembly and I win all the awards.

**TWO**. Beka and I hang out and her mom lets us stay up late so we can watch the meteor shower. We go down to the river and lay in the grass. Beka shows me my lymph nodes, her fingers crawling all over me – in my neck, my hips, next to my pubic bone, in my armpits next to my breasts... It's cloudy but we still see two shooting stars. What do I wish? That Josh will always be a part of my life. Twice. I wish that twice.

**FOUR**. Someone tells me that Josh had sex with Mikaela this beautiful half-deaf girl who had cancer as a baby and that's why he broke up with me and I start to cry

...

...

And then I just get very quiet

I've never been this quiet

On the inside

...

I'm so quiet it's almost as if I don't exist at all

> *ONE, TWO, THREE and FOUR project*
> *grotesque drawings from Clare's journal onto*
> *the walls...*

        ...

         ...

          ...

           ...

            ...

             ...

              ...

               ...

                ...

                ..

                .

sadness overwhelming
why is it so hard to love somebody

Blue Fox
My feet grew.
smell my smells the sour smell of sweat

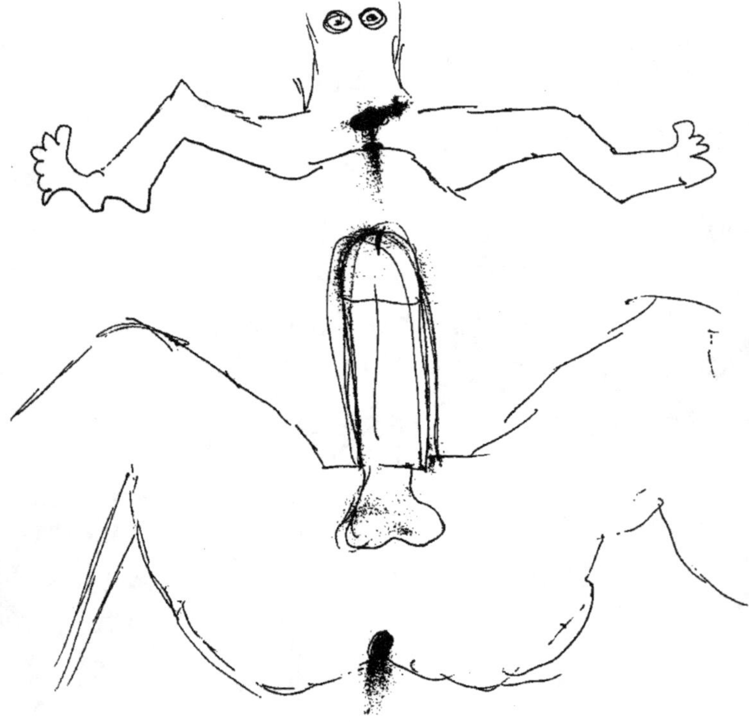

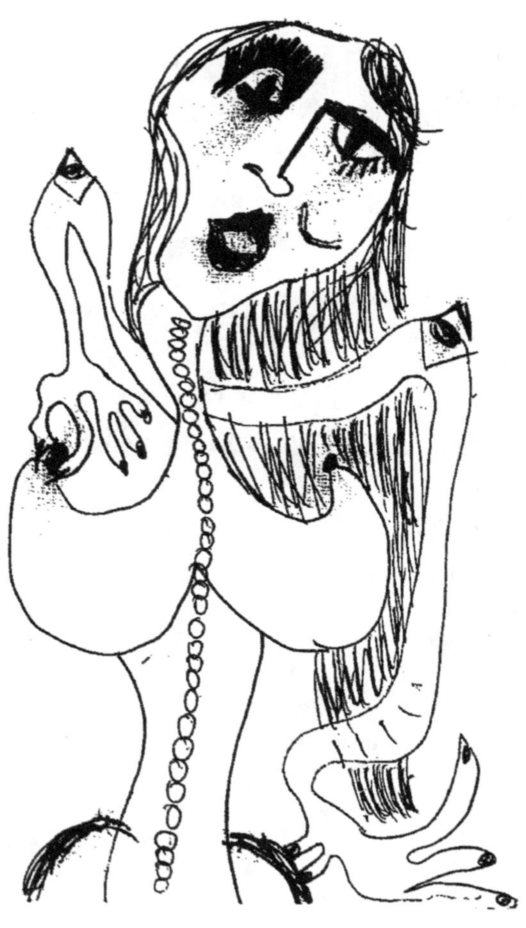

> *Two previously pretty quiet MEMBERS OF
> THE CHOIR – off-on-the-side – start making
> out.*

**GUY**. Hey

**CLARE**. Hey

**GUY**. You okay?

**CLARE**. Yeah

**GUY**. Are you going to look at me

**CLARE**. Sorry

**GUY**. I want to fuck you

**CLARE**. What?

**GUY**. I said, I want to fuck you. I find you very sexy

**CLARE**. *(Mumbles, stumbles, etc.)* Oh. Yeah, um I want to, too

**GUY**. We don't have to if you don't want to

**CLARE**. No, I want to

> *They return to furiously making out.*

**CLARE**. Just so you know

I haven't really done...that much...

**GUY**. Really?

**CLARE**. Yeah

**GUY**. I don't believe you

**CLARE**. It's true. I mean, I've done a lot, but not like...stuff

**GUY**. I feel like you're very experienced

> *She laughs.*
>
> *She shakes her head.*
>
> *She starts to secretly cry.*

**GUY**. Wait – So you and Josh didn't –?

**CLARE**. We sort of did our own thing

**GUY**. What's that mean

**CLARE**. I don't know

We like –

Took showers together

And did some rough stuff

**GUY**. What

**CLARE**. We did some rough stuff?

**GUY**. Really?

**CLARE**. Yeah. I don't know

> *They keep making out. Slowly, over the course of the following, he takes off her jeans.*

**CLARE**. Can I ask you a question?

**GUY**. Sure

**CLARE**. Do you believe in Heaven?

**GUY**. No

**CLARE**. Are you serious?

**GUY**. Yeah I don't believe in heaven

**CLARE**. I don't believe you

**GUY**. I don't

**CLARE**. Why not

**GUY**. I just think it's stupid

And obviously not true

**CLARE**. And you're okay with that?

**GUY**. Yeah

**CLARE.** You're okay with just dying? Just never existing again?

**GUY.** Yeah I'm okay with that

**CLARE.** How are you okay with that?

**GUY.** It's not that big of a deal

**CLARE.** I am not okay

**GUY.** Yeah?

**CLARE.** I am NOT OKAY with that at all

> *He slides her underwear over her hips. She reflexively stops him for a second, then lets him do it.*

**CLARE.** Do you believe in the Mayan Apocalypse?

**GUY.** *(Laughing.)* No

**CLARE.** You don't think we're all going to die in 2012??????

**GUY.** No. I do *not*

> *She's on her back. Her feet are on his chest. Then on his face.*

> *She puts one of them in his mouth.*

**CLARE.** My sister-in-law's sister read my palm and she told me that I'm either gonna die at twenty-six or forty and twenty-six is how old I'll be during the Mayan apocalypse...

> *He grabs her feet and puts them on either side of him. He starts to go down on her.*

**CLARE.** Hey, I'm scared

**GUY.** Don't worry, you're not going to die for a long, long time

**CLARE.** *(Mumbles.)* No I was talking about –

**GUY**.  Is this okay?

**CLARE**.  Yes

**GUY**.  Does it feel good?

> *She makes a face like: what the fuck.*

**CLARE**.  Yes

**GUY**.  *(Coming back up for air.)* What'd you say?

**CLARE**.  I said, it feels good

> *She squeezes him hard with her legs, and they start to wrestle. It gets a little vicious.*
>
> *He hits her really hard across the face.*

**CLARE**.  *whoa.*

> *He hits her really hard across the face again.*

   ...

   ...

   ...

   ...

   ...

   ...

**GUY**.  Do you like that?

**CLARE**.

   ...

   ...

> *She spits in his face.*

**CLARE**.  *(sorry!)*

> *They start to kiss again.*

**CLARE**.  I've never seen a penis before

> *She starts to laugh.*

**GUY**.  What?

**CLARE**.  I said, I've never seen a penis before

**GUY**.  Well get ready

> *He puts his finger inside of her.*

**GUY**.  Relax...

 ...

 ...

 ...

Relax

**CLARE**.  I am relaxing!

**GUY**.  No you're not, you have to relax

> *She tries to relax.*

> *He takes his fingers and puts them in his mouth and goes back to fingering her.*

**CLARE**.

 ...

 ...

 ...

 ...

It doesn't really hurt it just –

**GUY**.  How does that feel? Does that feel good?

**CLARE**.  It doesn't really feel like anything

**GUY**.  Just wait for it

> *He goes at her with his finger.*

> *She wants him to stop.*

**CLARE**.  I don't want to have sex tonight

**GUY**.  That's okay.

**CLARE**. Thanks

**GUY**. There's plenty of other things we can do

*He fucks her with her finger.*

**GUY**. Does that feel good?

*(Kinda?? Maybe?? Not really.)*

**GUY**. Oh my god

**CLARE**. What?

**GUY**. I just can't believe this is happening

*He fucks her furiously with his finger. He's really into it. But he's hurting her. She wants him to stop.*

*Slowly…*

**GUY**. Yes

Yes

Yes

YES

YES

YES

YES

YES

YES

YES!!!!!!!!!!

YES!!!!!!!!!

YES!!!!!!!!!!!

...

...

...

**FOUR.**  I never told Josh when I played the piano. Not once during our entire relationship. I didn't want him to feel obligated to come see me, or be unimpressed. But he called my house one night (probably about a month before we broke up) and by accident found out I was playing at the French Talent Show – onstage, under light. He and Scott rushed down and caught the very end of my song. We talked after – he had to go to a party at Alana's house and I had to go to Gavin's house with the Ashleys, Beka and Melissa. I felt guilty for abandoning those girls. I felt guilty for not missing them. We watched the movie *Signs* and Gavin played the guitar and I was happy because Josh was supposed to pick me up later and I felt very mature and special and very well-liked waiting amongst these people for my senior boyfriend. He was late. And when he finally arrived with Scott they grumbled that I had given them the wrong directions and they'd been searching forever. They were angry. I was ashamed and felt annoying. We went to Alana's and wasted time. Then we all drove back together to Josh's house listening to loud music. But by the time we got there it was my curfew. So Josh drove me home. I lay in his lap. And he stroked my hair, my back, my face. So safe. We kissed. Him coming down from above – taking forever to do it because I kept chickening out and avoiding eye contact to stare at the trees. And that was the first night I felt it. Laying in his lap. Seatbelt straps everywhere. His hand on my thigh – circling up. And all of a sudden my head was screaming: HIGHER HIGHER. It didn't feel lustful or dirty. Just like the most urgent thing in the world. And then his hand is on my butt. And it's like a siren in my head, screaming over-and-over again: higher higher, and firmer than before. And then he touched it. Over my jeans. And I still remember my shock. Utter disbelief. That anything could feel like that. The lower half of my body just floated away. It was as if I went numb and my nerves exploded simultaneously. I expanded. My vagina was on happy gas like at the dentist – floating, burning, tingling with cold, throbbing. And suddenly my mouth was desperate, digging into him all the while my body was floating away and I kept thrusting to catch up with my ghost body that was floating somewhere above my head. It felt so good and free and powerful. *I want it.*

**ONE.**

What I've learned is that you can never count on another person. You have to only count on yourself. Because you can lose another person. And then your whole world falls apart. So you can never make another person your entire world. Otherwise, you're going to lose your entire world. And that's so painful. That's too painful. That's not something you should really do unless you want to torture yourself. You just have to love with no expectation of anything in return. You just have to love to love to love to love to love to love to love and lose and lose and lose and lose and lose...

*Music plays as loud as possible over the loudspeakers. Propulsive and full of testosterone. Something that makes you feel sexy...*[*]

*Boom! Crack!
Boom–boom–boom!
Crack–crack!*

---

[*] A license to produce *I'll Never Love Again* does not include a performance license for any third-party or copyrighted music. Licensees should create an original composition or use music in the public domain. For further information, please see the Music and Third-Party Materials Use Note on page iii.

*The world transforms, and suddenly, we are in an office.*

*Somewhere cleverly hidden in the scenery is the date: December 21, 2012.*

*The sound of the printer. Somebody is printing something but they are nowhere in sight. We watch the paper come out of the printer.*

Ch-ch-ch-cheeee!

Ch-ch-ch-cheeee!

Ch-ch-ch-cheeee!

*Slowly we notice a WOMAN on the floor. She is surrounded by big black binders full of reams and reams of papers. She is hunched over these binders, on her knees. She is very focused – furrowed brow, reading softly under her breath... She holds a big black Sharpie* and is meticulously crossing things out.*

*The printer stops.*

*SOMEBODY appears and retrieves the printed papers. They leave. A MAN intersects with them in the background, going the opposite direction.*

*He returns and watches the woman on the floor. This is ROGER.*

*He kind of looks like a soldier on his way back from battle – his eyes bloodshot and sad.*

---

* A license to produce *I'll Never Love Again* does not include a license to publicly display any branded logos or trademarked images. Licensees must acquire rights for any logos and/or images or create their own.

*His body spent. But he's just a lawyer who's spent the last ten years of his life working way too hard.*

ROGER. Clare?!

CLARE. Oh, hey Roger!

ROGER. I didn't know you were here!

CLARE. Yeah they called me in / last night

ROGER. You here just for the day?

CLARE. No Amanda said it'd probably be / a couple of days

ROGER. Aw they got you with Amanda

CLARE. Yup

ROGER. I'm jealous

CLARE. I think she's pretty desperate

ROGER. No she is

*CLARE hasn't stopped working.*

ROGER. You want to sit at a table?

CLARE. No, that's / okay

ROGER. I can get you a table

CLARE. I actually like working on the floor

ROGER. You sure?

CLARE. Yeah I'm good

ROGER.

   …

   …

   …      *(He watches her.)*

   …

   …

**CLARE.** *(Just realizing.)* Oh, sorry! Am I in your way?

**ROGER.** No! You're fine.

…

…

I'm just deciding whether or not to make myself a cup of coffee. I think I just need to sit…for a minute.

**CLARE.** Just tell me if you want me to move

**ROGER.** Will do

> *ROGER perches somewhere. CLARE keeps working.*
>
> *ROGER looks at the snack station. He takes a bag of Fritos.* [*]

**ROGER.** I'm not supposed to have these

**CLARE.** Knock yourself out

> *He opens them and eats.*
>
> *A long-ish moment of CLARE redacting, ROGER eating Fritos…*
>
> *The printer starts up again.*
>
> *ROGER sighs.*

**ROGER.** Oh man

**CLARE.** You okay

**ROGER.** I just had a kind of awful phone call

**CLARE.** I'm sorry

**ROGER.** It doesn't matter. How are / you?

---

* A license to produce *I'll Never Love Again* does not include a license to publicly display any branded logos or trademarked images. Licensees must acquire rights for any logos and/or images or create their own.

**CLARE.** Uh-oh

**ROGER.** What

**CLARE.** I think I just crossed the wrong thing out

**ROGER.** Are you sure?

*CLARE stares despondently at the page.*

**CLARE.** *Ahhhhhhhh*

**ROGER.** See that's why you shouldn't talk to people while you're redacting

**CLARE.** *(Laughing.) Fuckkkkkkkkkk*

**ROGER.** Are you sure?

**CLARE.** Yes! *(Under her breath.)* Ahh... Now I have to reprint this page...

**ROGER.** The server's down

**CLARE.** What

**ROGER.** They've been having problems / with it all day, so none of the printers are working

**CLARE.** Okay

**ROGER.** You're going to have to email Mark and he'll print it for you

**CLARE.** But it's printing!

**ROGER.** I know, he's doing it from the admin

**CLARE.** Oh my god! Roger!

**ROGER.** Email Mark

*An existential cry. Tiny, under her breath, to the universe...*

**CLARE.** *I have to gooooooooooooooooooooooooooooooooooo*

*She looks down at the paper helplessly.*

*ROGER pulls a burnt Frito out of his chip bag.*

**ROGER.** Black Frito

**CLARE.** What?

**ROGER.** It's all burnt

**CLARE.** Oh

**ROGER.** Should I eat it

**CLARE.** I really have to email Mark?

**ROGER.** Yes

*ROGER contemplates the burnt Frito. And then eats it.*

*JACKSON pops his head in.*

**JACKSON.** Hey

**ROGER.** Hey

**JACKSON.** Have you seen Amanda?

**ROGER.** Try the conference room

**JACKSON.** Thanks

*CLARE has opened the binder, removed the mismarked piece of paper, and set it aside. It's very tragic.*

**CLARE.** It's kind of sad, you know

Going through these emails

The guy's going through a divorce

And then his wife *(under her breath)* <gets an abortion>

And they're emailing back-and-forth

It's like.........

...

...

I should not be seeing this

**ROGER.** The guy's a dick

**CLARE.** Makes me never want to write anything in an email ever again

...

...

> *AMANDA comes barreling in from the opposite direction and makes a beeline for the Keurig machine.*[*]

**AMANDA.** Have you seen Jackson?

**ROGER.** He was just looking for you

> *AMANDA looks at ROGER – utterly in despair.*

**AMANDA.** *(Mouthing the words.)* <He's driving me crazy>

**ROGER.** I know, I know

**AMANDA.** *<What the fuck is wrong with him?>*

**ROGER.** Honestly, Amanda, I don't know

**CLARE.** Oh, sorry! Am I in your way?

**AMANDA.** You're good

> *AMANDA is jabbing at the Keurig machine.*

**AMANDA.** Why isn't this working?

**ROGER.** Are you pushing the right button?

**CLARE.** I think you have to wait for the water to boil.

---

[*] A license to produce *I'll Never Love Again* does not include a license to publicly display any branded logos or trademarked images. Licensees must acquire rights for any logos and/or images or create their own.

**AMANDA.** *(To ROGER, teasing.)* How does she know that and not you?

**ROGER.** *(To himself.)* I always push the wrong button...

> *It takes a minute but then hot coffee comes streaming out. AMANDA leans against the counter and waits.*

**AMANDA.** How are you guys doing?

**CLARE.** I'm / fine

**ROGER.** We're good

**AMANDA.** *(To ROGER.)* Did you talk to Spivak?

**ROGER.** I did

**AMANDA.** What are you going to do about it?

**ROGER.** Nothing tonight. I have to leave at six

**AMANDA.** Uch. Don't tell me that

**ROGER.** I'm taking my daughter to a concert for the Mayan Apocalypse

| **AMANDA.** | **CLARE.** *(Yawning.)* |
|---|---|
| The Mayan Apocalypse! | Oh, cool! |

**ROGER.** Or not my daughter. My partner's daughter.

**CLARE.** *Oona.*

| **ROGER.** | **AMANDA.** |
|---|---|
| That's right. | What do they do at a concert for the Mayan Apocalypse? |

**CLARE.** I love that name

**ROGER.** She's really into Mayans and Aztecs and stuff so I thought it would be good.

**AMANDA.** What do they do at a concert for the Mayan / Apocalypse?

ROGER.  I don't know. Chanting? Singing? Apparently if you make it to midnight there's a survivors' dance party. But I don't think we're going to make it that long…

*AMANDA fixes her coffee – lots of Splenda.**

AMANDA.  How's that coming, Clare? You think you'll be done before eight?

CLARE.  I just have to reprint this one page

AMANDA.  The server's down

CLARE.  I know

AMANDA.  Email Mark he'll print it for you

| CLARE. | ROGER. *(To AMANDA.)* |
|---|---|
| Thanks | How's Mark doing by the way? |

AMANDA.  He's okay. Shelley was talking to him about it, and he was saying that he's finally feeling like himself again

| CLARE. | AMANDA. |
|---|---|
| What happened to Mark? | Which is good |

ROGER.  He was hit by a car / on his bike.

| CLARE. | AMANDA. |
|---|---|
| Oh my God | Apparently he's still got a big ol' bruise on his face |

ROGER.  And the driver didn't stop

CLARE.  *All my friends are going to die on bikes*

ROGER & AMANDA.  …

---

* A license to produce *I'll Never Love Again* does not include a license to publicly display any branded logos or trademarked images. Licensees must acquire rights for any logos and/or images or create their own.

**CLARE.**  Is he okay???

**AMANDA.**  He's totally fine. He's just really unnerved that someone would do that

**ROGER.**  He was laid up for awhile, though, wasn't he?

**AMANDA.**  No, I think he was fine. Just rattled

**ROGER.**  I thought it was a pretty bad accident...

**AMANDA.**  Just a bruise on his cheekbone, I think

**ROGER.**  Oh.

*ROGER is puzzled by this.*

**ROGER.**  Okay

**AMANDA.**  What?

**ROGER.**  No, I just misunderstood – I thought it was really bad

**AMANDA.**  Roger!

**ROGER.**  What?

**AMANDA.**  It *was* bad! Someone hit him with a car and drove away at three o'clock in the morning and just left him there lying on the street!

**ROGER.**  I just didn't realize he wasn't actually hurt!

*AMANDA looks at him.*

**ROGER.**  What?? That's a good thing!

**CLARE.**  I got hit by a car once

**ROGER.**  Really?

**CLARE.**  The day my grandfather died, and I knew the person who hit me –

**ROGER.**  Oh / wow

**AMANDA.**  Whoa

**CLARE.** And it was raining. And they wouldn't let me get up because they had to clear my spine first. So I was just lying there in the rain with my face in the concrete and all these people touching me and talking to me... And when they finally let me sit up, I was so surprised to see him, I was just like: *It's you!*

**AMANDA.** Who was he?

**CLARE.** Just some kid I went to school with. He was super embarrassed about it.

...

And then we ended up dating for three months!

| **AMANDA.** | **ROGER.** |
|---|---|
| Do you think you were attracted to him because of the accident? | Clare! |

**CLARE.** *(Laughing; tragic.)* Probably...

**ROGER.** My ex-wife accidentally slammed the car door on our oldest son's arm –

| **AMANDA.** | **CLARE.** |
|---|---|
| Oof | *Oh* |

**ROGER.** – when he was four and broke it in three places. I think she cried harder than he did...

**CLARE.** Oh my god, *of course*! I would hate myself

**AMANDA.** I think the worst thing I ever did... *Uch... I don't know if I can say this...* I accidentally killed my pet hamster. I was jumping on the bed –

**CLARE.** Oh no

**AMANDA.** And tossing him up into the air and catching him again

**CLARE.** Oh no, oh no

**AMANDA.** And he flew straight into the fan...

*ROGER and CLARE react.*

**AMANDA.**  And my mom made me clean it up

> *ROGER and CLARE are kind of laughing.*
> *AMANDA, too...*

**AMANDA.**  It's not funny. It's really not funny.

> ...
> ...          *The WOMEN start to really laugh.*
> ...
> ...          **ROGER.**
> ...              I know someone whose son died in the
> ...              propellor of a speedboat. He was swimming
> ...              and he just got sucked in
> ...
> ...
> ...

**AMANDA.**  I just keep thinking about his little beady eyes,
staring back at me. He must've felt so betrayed.

> *They get themselves under control.*

**AMANDA.**  No, but it's confusing when someone you love –
I had this crazy experience – *(To ROGER.)* – we've
talked about this – where I was sexually assaulted by a
stranger in college? And then afterwards, my boyfriend
at-the-time was kind of helping me get through it,
and like a week later... I went out with him. And I got
super high. And super drunk. Just like – raging. And
I must've passed out, because I remember waking up.
And he was having sex with me. And we hadn't – like
we hadn't gone there yet after the – because I hadn't
wanted to. But I guess that night he thought that
I wanted it? That's why we had gone out? But I didn't.
And I stopped being able to have sex with him. At all.
I mean, after that night. And we broke up. And I sort
of forgot about it. But I've been working on this case,

this Johnson kid case, and all-of-a-sudden I've been thinking about it again, like *what was going on? Like in his head?* Like I know he cared about me. But did he know? What he was doing, or... I don't know.

...

Shelley was saying I should send him a message on Facebook but I don't think I really want to do that...

**CLARE.** I don't think you have to do that if you don't want to...

> *JACKSON enters. He goes to the water cooler.*

**CLARE.** Hi Jackson

**JACKSON.** Hi

> *JACKSON drinks.*

**AMANDA.** *(To JACKSON.)* Do you still need me?

**JACKSON.** Do you have a second?

**AMANDA.** Uhhh sure

Just give me a minute and I'll come find you

**JACKSON.** Sounds good

> *He goes. CLARE hands AMANDA a piece of paper from her redaction binder for AMANDA's review.*

**CLARE.** (Is this alright?)

> *AMANDA scans it. Both of the WOMEN dissolve back into their respective tasks.*

**ROGER.** Ahh. I should get back to work

> *ROGER starts to move – maybe to throw away his cup. He laughs to himself.*

**ROGER.** I'm doing this counseling thing with my partner.

**CLARE.**  Oona's mom.

**ROGER.**  Yeah. And I had to uh

I had to write down the biggest traumas of my life

**CLARE.**  Uh-huh

**ROGER.**  And I thought I would write about my divorce or getting sober or something like that. But I found myself writing about my sister and the day I left for college. And when we said goodbye, she started crying, like sobbing hysterically, and my parents made me get in the car because I had to catch my plane. And I remember looking behind me, and my sister was still crying like that, pretty much having a panic attack in the middle of our driveway, and as the car drove away, she started to chase the car, down the street, reaching out her arms, like: *Don't goooo*

...

...

...		*ROGER is cosmically amused by the image*
...		*of his sister chasing the car...*

...

...

...

And so I called my sister, because that's what you're supposed to do, you're supposed to call the people you write about, and I said: Nancy! I am *so sorry* we left you alone like that, that we didn't take you with us, or I don't know, *wait*. And she started laughing. And she said: Roger... I have absolutely no idea what you're talking about. Anyway. Why am I telling you this?

**CLARE.**  *(Kind of laughing.)* I don't / know

**AMANDA.**  *(Kind of laughing.)* Why are you telling us?

*He smiles at them.*

**ROGER.**  Something to say

*AMANDA and ROGER exit.*

*OONA appears. She is thirteen years old. She wears a backpack.*

**OONA**. Hi

**CLARE**. Oh, hi! Are you Oona?

**OONA**. Yeah

**CLARE**. I'm so happy to meet you!

*OONA is slightly weirded out by this.*

**CLARE**. You want me to go get your dad

**OONA**. He's not my dad

**CLARE**. I mean Roger

**OONA**. No it's okay. I texted him

*OONA slings off her backpack.*

**CLARE**. Do you want a chair or something?

**OONA**. Um. Sure

*CLARE gets OONA a chair. OONA sits.*

**OONA**. Thanks

**CLARE**. No problem

*CLARE goes back to work on the floor. OONA watches her.*

**OONA**. What are you doing?

**CLARE**. I'm doing something called redaction

**OONA**. Why are you working on the floor?

**CLARE**. I like it

**OONA**. Don't you have a desk?

**CLARE.**  I actually don't have a desk here

**OONA.** Oh

**CLARE.**  Or not an official desk

**OONA.** Cool

   …

   …

   …

What's redaction?

**CLARE.**  Oh. Ummm. It's where you cover up everything that's not really relevant to the matter at hand

**OONA.**  Can I see?

**CLARE.**  Sure

*OONA crawls over to CLARE.*

**CLARE.**  Or actually, not this page. One sec –

*CLARE flips through the binder to find something appropriate.*

**CLARE.**  So, look –

This whole email is just like: *this is what I'm having for dinner*

**OONA.**  Uh-huh

**CLARE.**  And that doesn't have anything to do with whether or not he stole a bunch of money. So I cross it out and then that way the courts don't invade his privacy

**OONA.**  Uh-huh

*OONA thinks about this for a second.*

**OONA.**  What if he stole the money so he could have a really nice dinner

**CLARE.**  Ummm

I don't think that's what happened…

**OONA.** Is his life over?

**CLARE.** You mean like –

**OONA.** Is he going to jail for the rest of his life?

**CLARE.** I'm not sure. Maybe

**OONA.** Do you like him?

**CLARE.** Um... Not really

*CLARE closes the binder.*

**CLARE.** Anyway

**OONA.** Thanks for showing me

**CLARE.** You're welcome

*CLARE stays sitting on the floor next to OONA. She's tired.*

**CLARE.** How's eighth grade going

**OONA.** How do you know I'm in eighth grade

**CLARE.** Roger told me

**OONA.** He talks about me?

**CLARE.** Yeah

*OONA takes this in.*

**OONA.** I don't know. It kind of sucks

**CLARE.** Are you excited for high school?

*She shrugs.*

**OONA.** I'm not really thinking about it

**CLARE.** Roger says you're on the high school swim team already

**OONA.** Yeah

**CLARE.** That's cool

**OONA.** …

**CLARE.** …

**OONA.** …

**CLARE.** High school's going to be way better than middle school

**OONA.** Yeah…

**CLARE.** You'll see

**OONA.** I'm a little scared

**CLARE.** Of high school?

**OONA.** Yeah

**CLARE.** Don't be scared

**OONA.** I know

**CLARE.** You're gonna love it

**OONA.** Yeah

**CLARE.** Or you're gonna hate it

It doesn't matter

A lot of stuff is going to happen

It'll be great

**OONA.** I know

**CLARE.** …

**OONA.** …

**CLARE.** …

**OONA.** Did you like high school?

**CLARE.** It was alright

*They sit.*

**CLARE.** Just don't be scared to have an opinion, okay

That's the one thing I would say

**OONA.**  Yeah I'm not

**CLARE.**  Everyone is stupid. Except for you

Remember that

And it's okay to be angry

Like if you're angry

Be angry!

That's totally okay

**OONA.**  …

**CLARE.**  And do whatever you want

But don't stay with someone who's mean to you

You're going to want to stay with them…

Because they're older or you think they're cool

But if someone's mean to you –

Just walk away

**OONA.**  …

**CLARE.**  Sorry. I don't mean to tell you what to do…

**OONA.**  No, it's okay. I already knew most of that stuff anyway

**CLARE.**  …

**OONA.**  I would never be with someone who was mean to me. Are those snacks?

**CLARE.**  Yeah. You want some?

**OONA.**  Sure

*They go over to the snack area.*

**OONA.**  Can I have Cheetos?

**CLARE.**  Take as many as you want

*They load her up.*

**OONA.** Is that a coffee machine?

**CLARE.** Yeah, it's called a Keurig

**OONA.** It looks like a spaceship

**CLARE.** Are you a coffee drinker?

**OONA.** My mom says I have to wait until college

**CLARE.** *(Slightly amused by this.)* I don't really remember when I started drinking coffee...?

Maybe it was college?

>        *CLARE looks at her a little mischievously.*

**CLARE.** You want to try a little bit?

**OONA.** Sure

>        *CLARE pushes the buttons on the Keurig machine. ROGER walks in.*

**ROGER.** Hello, hello!

**CLARE.** Hi Roger

**ROGER.** You ready to go

**OONA.** Yeah

**ROGER.** Wait. Do I have my phone? *(To OONA.)* Is that what you're wearing?

**OONA.** Yeah

**ROGER.** Aren't you cold?

**OONA.** No

**CLARE.** Goodnight, Oona

Enjoy the concert

**OONA.** Goodnight! Nice to meet you!

**ROGER.** Goodnight, Clare

**CLARE.** Goodnight

*They're gone.*

*Oona's coffee has finished brewing. CLARE
looks at it. She pours it into the garbage.*

*The world melts.*

### THREE.

And so I began my twenty-sixth year of life
I didn't notice the revolution initially
It was gradual and subtle
I formed a tender and strange affection
for the very things that used to haunt me
The fuzz inside my ass cheeks
My dopey nipples
The rogue, random hairs
The way my skin was already falling
down and becoming less elastic...

I stopped washing my body
I stopped brushing my hair
I could smell my pussy everywhere I went

Layer upon layer of secretions and sweat
I masked it all with perfume

And big box-sack dresses that I stopped
washing
I slept on the floor in a nest with my cats
I only loved people who gave me food
And the love only lasted as long as the
eating
I stopped drinking alcohol
I stopped drinking coffee
I stopped running when there was no
real reason to run other than genuine joy
or genuine fear and I started taking long
walks through the neighborhood

**THREE.**

Things fell apart
People left
People I loved died
Bad things happened
People did bad things to my body
I sometimes was very mean and ungenerous
The state of our country got very bad
Everyone was very tired

The more my body fell apart the more I
loved it
The more I felt it was mine
And the more I wanted to fuck
And be seen
And be bent in all directions
And the more I wanted to sit with it quietly
Naked and alone in my apartment
Making eggs
Or eating spinach out of a bag with my
fingers
Each year was more thrilling than the last
Each year I understood more songs
I'd hear a song on the radio – a familiar
song, a song I'd heard a million times
before – and suddenly I'd go: Oh! So *that's*
what that song means

And each year I remembered songs I had
forgotten, ancient songs from childhood
that I used to sing when we were driving
around the city, doing our errands, me in the
backseat of the car, quietly singing under my
breath, and now I was singing them again,
quietly under my breath, as I walked through
the neighborhood, songs about birds and
bridges and rowboats and spiders

I stopped looking at people like they were *people*. And I started looking at them like they were *trees*

Everyone looked much more beautiful that way. And aging wasn't as scary

And I stopped worrying about love at all

*ROGER and OONA at the concert for the Mayan Apocalypse. It's an outdoor concert, and they're bundled up in coats. We hear some sort of guttural, pagan singing that slowly builds...*

**[MUSIC NO. 06 – WAYFARING STRANGER (APOCALYPSE VERSION)]**

**ROGER.** Are you nervous?

**OONA.** About what?

**ROGER.** That the world is going to end

**OONA.** No

**ROGER.** Not even a little?

**OONA.** Nope

**ROGER.** It's kind of fun to be afraid...

**OONA.** There's not even any Mayans here

**ROGER.** No. But I think there's going to be some dancing later...

*They try to see over the crowd.*

**ROGER.** You think you'd ever want to do something like this

**OONA.** Like what

**ROGER.** Sing in the choir

**OONA.** No

**ROGER.** Why not

**OONA.** I don't like singing

**ROGER.** How can someone not like singing

**OONA.** I don't know. I just don't

**ROGER.** I don't know. Now's the time in your life when it's good to try new things…

**OONA.** No

**ROGER.** No?

**OONA.** I know exactly what I want

**ROGER.** You do?

**OONA.** And nobody's going to make me do anything I don't want

**ROGER.** And what do you want, or you're not going to tell me that

**OONA.** I don't want to sing in the choir

**ROGER.** I gathered

**OONA.** I want to do sports

**ROGER.** Swimming, or –

**OONA.** Not just swimming

**ROGER.** What kind of sports

**OONA.** I don't care

**ROGER.** You don't

**OONA.** The ONLY THING I KNOW

Is that I love soccer!
And softball!
And swimming!

And volleyball!

And color!

And passion!

And risks!

And devouring life!

And dreaming and really believing with every ounce it could come true!

And crying!

And wild fantasies!

And the strength of the human spirit!

And something so great we can't understand it!

*Over the course of OONA's speech the CHOIR has grown and grown and grown – all the faces we remember from Act I – until they are singing full-out and OONA has to shout over them to be heard, her face burning bright!*

*She cuts them off.*

And love!
And sacrifice!

# And sports!
# And sports!
# And sports!!!!!

**End**

www.ingramcontent.com/pod-product-compliance
Lightning Source LLC
Chambersburg PA
CBHW070358120726
47909CB00008B/2909